How to Make Slime, Putty & Liquid Rainbows

Simple DIY Recipes

By

Denise Clark

Published by:

www.Valenciapub.com

Valencia Publishing House
P.O. Box 548
Wilmer, Alabama 36587

Cover & Interior designed

By

Heather Summers

First Edition

TABLE OF CONTENTS

Part 1

How to Make Slime

INTRODUCTION TO SLIME MAKING

SLIME is one of the best activities for kids out there. As a parent of two kids under ten, I can say with certainty that slime is not only a great sensory activity, but it also provides hours of entertainment at a reasonably low cost.

As far as toys go, slime is pretty easy to clean up (if you know how to do it!), and as long as you contain it to a tiled or laminate area, you shouldn't have any problems sorting it out. As an added bonus, the mess made while playing with slime can lead to a pretty fun bath routine, which is always a plus in our house.

In this part of the book, we've compiled our top 11 slime recipes, as well as a few great ideas for play with slime! And don't worry if your recipe goes wrong, because we've included some great trouble-shooting advice to go with all the slimy goodness.

So have fun, prepare to get messy and I'll see you in the recipes below.

RECIPE 1- GLITTER SLIME

OKAY, to start with, we're going to talk about creating a great slime which will be a hit with boys and girls alike. If you have younger kids, it is always a pretty good idea to keep them away from inedible slimes like this one. I'm talking about children who are younger than 18 months, generally speaking. That said, this sparkly slime is pretty hard to resist (even I think it's great to play with!)

This recipe will call for two supplies, and then a few added extra ingredients if you want some more color and sparkle.

Supplies:

- School Glue (clear is best)
- Liquid starch (or laundry soap)
- Food coloring
- Lots of chunky glitter!

How to do it:

No matter how well you follow the directions, you will probably find some deviation in the results. This is fine, and you shouldn't worry about it too much. Just adjust it to your needs until you have the slime that you want. That said, our directions will create a pretty good guideline to follow.

5oz of school glue is a pretty good start in regards to mixing up the batch. If you then add the same amount (start with a little less and go from there) of liquid starch, then you should have a pretty good base for your slime.

Once you have mixed all of this up, you should have a rubbery, oozy consistency. When you've mixed it all up, you can add a little food coloring until it is the color that you want. Throw in your glitter (more glitter for more sparkle!), and you should be done.

Keep in mind that you will have to do a fair bit of mixing in order to get a nice, even color. If you want to make this a little easier, just add the food coloring to the liquid starch and mix that up before you add it to the glue. This works if you want an easier time of getting even color, but playing with the slime for a while will make sure that you have it all mixed through anyway.

The chunky glitter and clear glue will make sure you have a translucent effect, with big glitter pieces "floating" around in the slime. This is really cool for playing with and has a pretty awesome effect.

You can play with this slime right away if you like, or you can leave it for a little while in order to make sure it gets a bit of extra stretchy texture. In fact, if you keep it in an airtight container, you should be able to keep this slime for several weeks, which is pretty great for play. It is easy to wipe off wood, tiles, plastic and so much more, so it's easy enough to play with if you pick a good spot.

Using chunky glitter will also help with cleaning up (you won't get fine glitter sticking to everything.).

All in all, this is a pretty good recipe for simple, sparkly fun.

Here is a cute video of making glitter slime, I thought it is a cute video, take a look

https://www.youtube.com/watch?v=X4wjRRdrJQw

RECIPE 2- LAVA SLIME

IF YOU are interested in adding some variation to your slime, then you will love the Hot Lava style slime in this recipe. It is a great recipe for imaginative play and is great for use with small plastic figures or other toys. It is made using several a few different colors of slime which, when mixed together, create a molten lava effective. It is a great way to spice things up and it really helps increase imaginative play. My kids really loved playing with little figures in the slime. It is pretty easy to do too, which is a huge bonus!

You start off by making four separate batches of your favorite slime. You need to make sure you add different colorings to each batch. Our recommended colors are gold (with glitter!), orange, yellow and red.

Supplies

- 5 oz. of clear glue
- Food coloring
- 4 oz. of Liquid starch
- Water
- Glitter! (Especially gold glitter)

How to do it:

Mix all of this together really well, changing the color for each batch of slime. For the gold slime, use yellow food coloring with a small dash of orange, and a lot of gold colored glitter, to make for a really spectacular looking slime!

Set all of these out where you would like to play with them. This can be in a bucket or tub, on a large table or on the tile floor. Then the fun starts!

One great activity is to see how long it takes your plastic toys to sink into the slime (or lava!). This can be great fun for any age, though you should watch younger kids to make sure that none of the slime is ingested.

Once play begins, stretching and playing with the slime will happen automatically. This creates a beautifully swirly, gorgeous pattern, which looks a lot like molten lava. Sometimes the slime will bubble, which just looks great with all of the colors and makes things so much more fun.

If you play with this slime for a while, you will undoubtedly find that the slime will all mix together and you will no longer have the molten lava effect that you started with. However, that's not a huge drawback, as it still looks beautifully sparkly and orange.

Again, clean-up is pretty easy if you keep your slime on wood, plastic, glass or tiles. Avoid fabrics and carpets if possible, and clean it all up with soap and water. We tried to keep this one contained to a big tub, but that didn't really work out, so we still had a lot of cleaning up to do! That said, it was pretty easy, and it was most definitely worth it!

Here is a video on how to make Lava Slime, but instead of using contact solution and baking soda, just use liquid corn starch. I think you will enjoy this video as it shows how vibrant the lava slime colors can be, take a look.

https://www.youtube.com/watch?v=wuPLUGNV8y4

RECIPE 3- NATURAL SLIME

WE'VE done two recipes so far, but most of them just don't work for little kids who still like to put everything in their mouths. So, if you have a young child who just can't stop tasting everything, then this might be the solution you have been looking for. This particular recipe only relies on one core ingredient, which is non-toxic, and pretty simple to use.

This one has no borax, no liquid starch, no laundry detergent and no other dangerous compounds. Best of all, it is easy and quick to make!

Supplies:

- Psyllium Husk (Metamucil will work if you don't mind an orange slime!)
- Water

How to do it:

Essentially, you need to find a natural finger supplement and boil it, along with the recommended amount of water on the packet, for 5 minutes, stirring to mix it all up. This should settle into a really nice slime that you can play with for hours. It is natural, good for your kids and if they eat it, they won't get sick.

Of course, it is probably not a great idea to eat huge amounts of fiber if you do not want to end up in the toilet for hours, but at least it is not poisonous!

So enjoy this simple, non-toxic slime and remember that you should not use Metamucil unless you are happy with orange slime. The regular, clear Metamucil doesn't work very well for this, so you need to pick another supplement if you want to do different colored slime.

RECIPE 4- PUMPKIN SPICE

SOMETIMES you just want a slime that is a little bit different from the normal slimes that you find on the internet. In my research to find the very best slime recipes for my kids, I came across the idea of using food spices to make a richer, more grown up smelling slime. This inspired me to try a pumpkin slime recipe, which is a lovely smelling slime that is a lot of fun too. It's a pretty basic recipe, which we then spice up a little (excuse my terrible puns!).

Supplies:

- ½ Cup Liquid starch
- A pumpkin
- ½ Cup Glue
- Pumpkin spices

How to do it:

This is a pretty easy recipe to make, and it doesn't take a lot of work. Make your usual slime, by combining starch and glue into a simple slime. Then, cut off the top of your pumpkin and scrape all of the insides out. Take out the seeds and mix about half of the scraped-out pumpkin with the rest of your slime mix, making sure to blend well.

After this, it is a pretty simple process of mixing in and blending the pumpkin spices well, to make sure that the slime smells and looks amazing. It will be a pretty bright colored orange at this point, and it will smell good enough to eat! Just make sure that you keep it away from little ones who might be tempted to put it into their mouths, as this is definitely not an edible recipe. It is also important to note that you should add at least 3 Table Spoons of spices to really make it smell good.

After you have mixed it all up, put it to one side in a bowl or something similar, and let it sit. This is a good way to make sure that it really sets well, and just makes it better. You should aim to let it set for at least 10 minutes, but you can do it for a lot longer if you keep it covered in something air tight.

You can add the seeds if you want a bit of extra texture to the slime, but that is pretty optional. It depends on what works best for you and your kids.

I found that this slime has a pretty great texture. It really oozes, and it's not overly rubbery, but my kids still really loved it, and had a lot of fun playing and making messes with it! Because it is more liquidy, it is better to play with this over a tiled area, or outside, so you can minimize the risk of making a big mess on a carpeted floor. It's pretty stretchy too, even though it's not too rubbery, and it makes a great activity for kids.

When it comes to storage, it is helpful to store this in an airtight container in the fridge. Keep in mind that this contains raw vegetable matter, so it can only store for about a week before it will start turning bad, and you don't want your kids to play with stuff that is starting to go off, of course.

As an alternative, you could just add a lot of spices and a little bit of orange food coloring, instead of adding the pumpkin itself. This will negate the texture and some of the lovely smell, but it should keep for a lot longer.

Whichever method you use, we hope you have a lot of fun with it!

RECIPE 5- SIMPLE SLIME

THE next recipe is an amazing way to combine the most simple ingredients (which we have covered in previous recipes), but still, make it fun and new for your kids. This recipe focused on making slime that was translucent instead of being a block of color. This means that there are more opportunities to play with the slime outside, on lightboxes, held up to the sky and so much more. It gives a new range of play options, so I felt that I just had to include it!

SUPPLIES:

- ½ cup of liquid starch
- ½ cup of clear glue
- Food coloring

HOW TO DO IT:

This is a pretty easy recipe, which makes it a great experience when you need to whip something up in quite a hurry. You know, for those days where the kids are just being crazy and are in no mood to do any of the activities that you have planned? Yeah, this is great for those days.

Mix food coloring into the liquid starch, making sure that it had been mixed evenly. Then, mix the glue into the mixture until everything is mixed really well together. It's a really easy recipe to follow, and that is part of what I adore about it! Once I have mixed this through, I like to let it sit for a bit, just like I do with most of my slime recipes. This just makes it extra sticky and rubbery and makes for a fantastic slime.

One thing about this recipe that does take a lot more time is the process of mixing it until it is the perfect slime consistency. While mixing it up is pretty quick, it takes a lot longer to mix it into the perfect slime. That said, this is something that the kids can do while they are playing with it. The way they grab and squeeze and stretch slime is a far better mixer than anything I can do!

This means that it is still a pretty easy recipe, and pretty quick, as the kids will have plenty of fun playing with the slime until it feels right. It also makes it a pretty good sensory activity, which I am all over!

If you find that it is too sticky, then you might have to add more starch. The slime itself stores really well in a simple container, as long as you make sure that it is pretty air tight. This is a slime that you can store for quite a few weeks and is really great to have on hand for when your kids are feeling bored. It is quite easy to clean too, as you only need soap and water to get it off your skin.

Because it is so translucent, it is great to play with, and it is actually a beautiful slime, especially since it is such a simple one to make.

RECIPE 6- EDIBLE SLIME

A LOT of the recipes that we have covered have not been edible ones, which is a shame for the little kids who would like to join in the fun. We have one natural recipe on this list, and I thought that it was only fair that I found a second one. The first one can take some time, and you have to either boil it over the stove or in the microwave. This is an excellent recipe, but it can take time, especially when you have little ones around you.

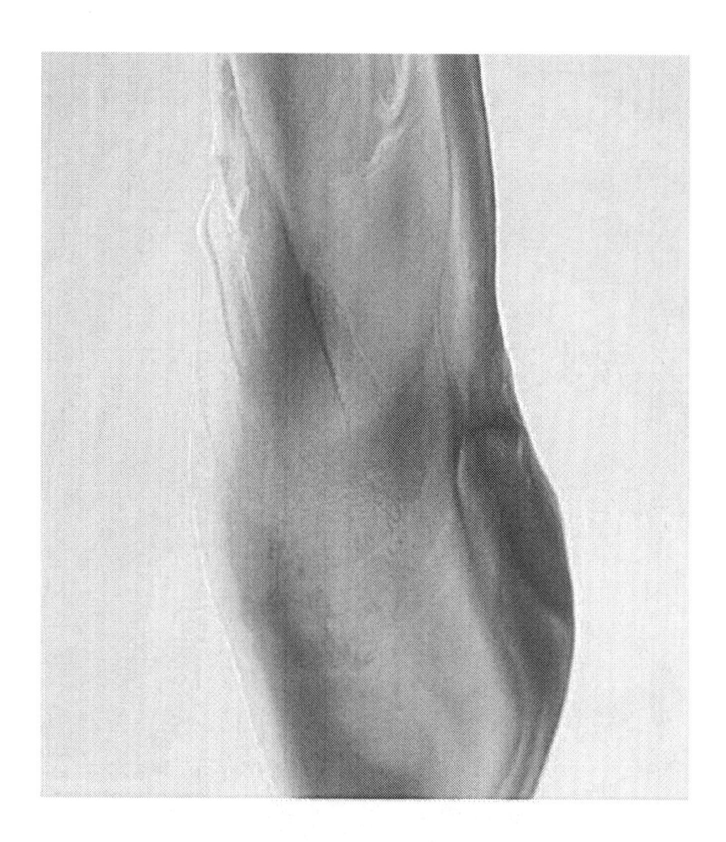

So in this recipe, we have simplified it yet again. Hopefully, this helps all you hard working parents out there who need a delicious edible slime recipe fast!

SUPPLIES:

- 16 oz. Corn-starch
- Food coloring
- 2.5 cups Water
- ¼ cup Basil seed

HOW TO DO IT:

The process itself is pretty straightforward, in that you just need to mix it all together! Mix the basil seeds and the cornstarch together, making sure that you break up the seeds and really mix it all together quite well. If you would like to have a colored slime, then you need to add the coloring to the water. Once you have done that, you need to add the water to the basil seed and cornstarch mixture. After this, it is just the process of mixing it all together over and over again until it is really well mixed.

This is a great activity for the kids to do, as they can mix it with their hands and really play with the slime while it is being mixed. Mixing is really key to making this recipe work, and it can be a lot of fun to do.

Keep in mind that this recipe contains safe edible products, and you need to store it in the fridge to make sure that it does not go bad. It should keep for about a week, much like the pumpkin spice slime. Then you will need to throw it away and make a new slime.

My kids really loved playing with this, and it was a tremendous peace of mind to know that they would not get sick if they ate some of it. That made the whole process pretty worthwhile, and I am sure that most parents of smaller children will definitely agree with me on that one.

So have fun and relax- you don't have to keep such a close watch on the kids while they play with this particular batch!

RECIPE 7- FLUFFY SLIME

IF YOU are looking for a slime that is a little bit less traditional, and a little bit more interesting for your kids, then this recipe might be the recipe that you have been looking for. It has an amazing texture, unlike any of the other slimes that we have experimented with in the past. Kids can get pretty bored with traditional slime, and this is a good way to make sure that the interest is kept alive.

Please keep in mind that this is definitely not an edible slime and that you need to make sure that your younger kids are not exposed to it in a way that they might be tempted to put it into their mouths.

Supplies:

- 2 tsp Glue
- ¼ cup Liquid starch
- Food Coloring
- ½ cup Shaving Cream

How to do it:

The process of making this slime is a pretty simple one. Just mix it all together, and you will have a fluffy, stretchy, amazingly textured slime which is sure to be a hit with your kids. It is like grabbing shaving cream, but it stretches and slips around just like a slime.

My kids had so much fun playing with it, and there were so many activities that we could do with it. We played with plastic toys in the slime, we grabbed it and stretched it and tried to pile it into cups. It was so much fun, and the best part of it is how easy it was to do. Most slimes are very exact, I have found. This one, though, is a very forgiving recipe and it is so much fun to play with and to make.

This will definitely be a hit in our home for some time!

I'm not sure how long this slime will keep since this was the first time I have made it, but I believe it will last for at least a few days, maybe longer, as long as we store it in an airtight container. It is easy to wash off too, and you can color it almost any color you like, as the shaving cream absorbs the color really well and makes it beautiful and vivid!

I definitely recommend this one if you are looking for a break from the usual slime recipes, and you think your kids would benefit from a bit of extra-sensory activity. I believe it is a fantastic one, and personally, even I had a lot of fun playing with it- the texture really is great once you get used to how unusual it is to have fluffy slime.

I hope you and your kids enjoy this recipe as much as we did!

RECIPE 8- BUBBLING SLIME

BUBBLING slime is one of the most amazing recipes that I have ever discovered! No, really. I am always looking for new and inventive slime recipes to keep my kids entertained, which is why I was so happy to find the fluffy slime recipe.

This one is just as interesting, and it captivated my kid's attention for hours, which is a pretty impressive feat all on its own. This recipe makes slime that continues to bubble for up to 24 hours and is a fantastic way to combine science, sensory play, and fun, to make sure that your kids get the very best of all that sensory play has to offer.

It combines slime, vinegar, and bicarb to make an amazing bubbly mix that is just so much fun to play with. It works best when you play with it in a tub so that the reaction can work probably.

You can't really move this slime a lot until the bubbling reaction is finished, or you won't get the full 24 hours. That said, you can still experiment, poke and prod it, play with it and use figurines to engage in imaginative play. These are all really powerful ways to play with slime.

This slime is technically edible, and it does not contain any poisons or chemicals, but it is not really advised for your child to consume a lot of the xanthan gum, so you need to watch your children, especially younger ones, just to make sure that your children are safe.

SUPPLIES:

- Baking soda
- 1 ¼ teaspoons of xanthan gum
- 2 cups of vinegar
- Food coloring

HOW TO DO IT:

Start this recipe by putting the vinegar in a bowl. Once you have done this, it is a slow process of gradually adding xanthan gum while you whisk it into the vinegar mixture. You need to really whisk this well and make sure that everything is really well mixed. You can add food coloring if you like, it is entirely up to you.

Unfortunately, this slime takes quite a few hours to set enough to play with it, and you need to put it in the fridge for at least 2 hours, maybe even more. This allows the xanthan to hydrate properly. Once you have given it a good amount of time to set, you need to whisk it again to make sure that it is smooth and ready to play with.

If it is too thick, add a little more vinegar. Aside from needing a lot of whisking, the rest of the process is quite simple. Just grab a sturdy tub that your kids can play with, and cover the bottom of the tub with the baking soda. Make sure that you cover it well, and as evenly as possible, but it is not an exact science.

Once you have done that, simply tip the slime over the baking soda and let it fill the tub up.

The reaction between the vinegar and the bicarb is what will cause the bubbles to form in your slime. Since the slime is a much thicker substance, thanks to the gum, it will take a lot longer for the reaction to form, which in turn creates long-lasting bubbles that are amazing to play with, and make the best sensory play tubs.

Storage for this is pretty simple, much like the rest of the slimes. It needs to be stored in an airtight container, within the fridge. Remember, like a few slimes we have covered in this book, this contains edible ingredients, so it probably won't be okay for more than a week. After that, it will start to turn bad, so it is important to get rid of the slime before that happens.

This slime is fantastic to play with, though, and it really does add to the experience. Once it has finished bubbling, you can still play with it in the same way you would normal slime. This means that it is pretty versatile and can really lead to hours and hours of play.

If you are looking for another, interesting slime to take your play to the next level, then this might be the slime you should try. Good luck and have fun- the possibilities are endless!

RECIPE 9- RAINBOW SLIME

RAINBOW slime is another great way to mix up the traditional slime recipe. This recipe calls for the very basic mix of glue and starch, which we have covered in the previous recipes. The change here is that we are now focusing on bringing out the best colors in order to make a big batch of rainbow slime. This is an excellent way to learn about color theory and to mix colors together.

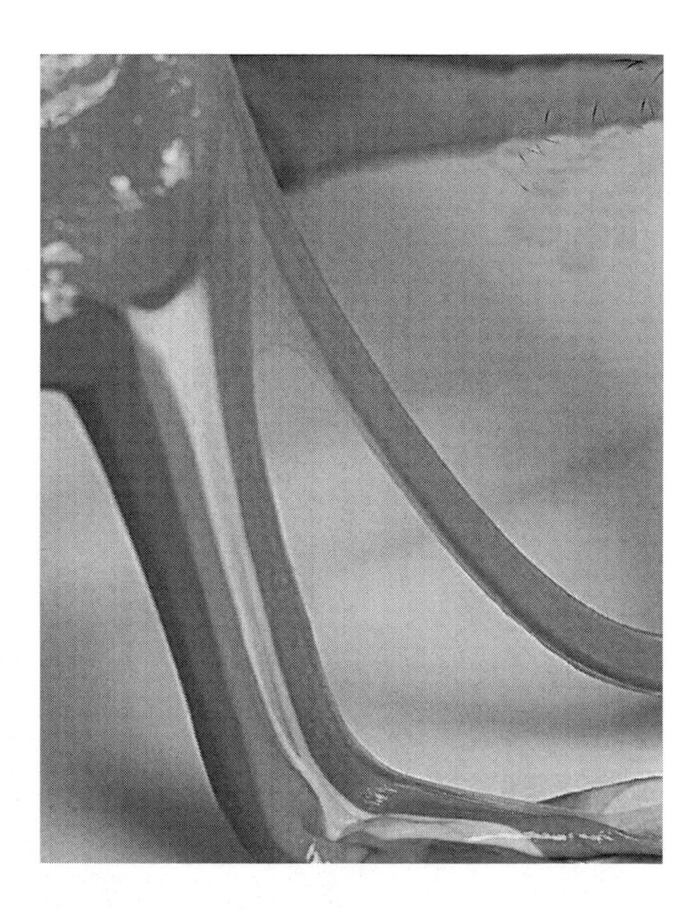

Supplies:

- 1 cup of clear glue
- 1 cup liquid starch
- Food coloring

How to do it:

Much like the recipes before, all you need to do is mix everything up together really, really well! One way to do this is to get the kids to play with it before it is fully mixed and let them help with the mixing, as mixing it by hand is the best way to do it. Mix a whole batch up without adding any food coloring. Once you have done a good job mixing it all up, then you can divide it into lots of little bowls and add the food coloring.

Pay extra attention not to stain your hands as you mix the food coloring in. By using clear glue, the colors are going to pop really nicely, which looks gorgeous when it comes down to it.

This can take a little while, and it is always best to let it set for at least ten minutes before you play with it.

To get started, you might want to set out all the different colored slimes for your children to play with and really get a good look at them.

This is where you can start making time to play with the slime and experiment with color. Break off little bits of the slime and mix different colors together to find out what color combinations do what. This is an excellent way for children to play with slime and learn about color at the same time.

You should store this slime in airtight containers, and since the slime is pretty stable, you shouldn't have any problem with it going bad. In fact, it should last for at least a few weeks, if not longer. It is a pretty versatile slime, and even if all of the colors end up mixing together, they will still make a pretty awesome slime, even if the color changes.

All up, this is a great slime for teaching kids about colors, while embracing the beauty of vivid color and bright slim, which is just so much fun to play with, that it is pretty hard to ignore.

Just a quick warning, though, this is not an edible slime, so watch what you do when you are playing with your little ones. It is good to supervise this activity and keep it away from very young kids.

RECIPE 10- GALAXY SLIME

WE HAVE all seen the pretty glitter slimes on the internet and admired how lovely they look. I even included one with nice, chunky bits of glitter at the very beginning of this book. It is safe to say that kids love glitter, so it is always a big hit. In this recipe, we take it a step further, including a number of different colors and glitters that allow for a slime that shines just like the night sky.

It is important to use very, very fine glitter to start with, as this gives a more realistic look which the chunky glitter just does not manage in the same way. That said, you can still include some bigger glitter pieces for added definition and sparkle in your slime creation. It is also important to really consider what colors best mimic the night sky. Colors like silver, black, purple and blue are really great for creating this slime.

The recipe itself is pretty basic, but you will be surprised at how gorgeous it looks when it is finished!

SUPPLIES:

- 5oz clear glue
- Food coloring
- ½ cup liquid starch
- Lots of fine glitters!

How to do it:

This slime works best if you take things nice and slowly. Start by adding the glue and then slowly put in the liquid starch. Do it slowly, mixing all the while, until you have the consistency that you want. Once you have done this, you should start mixing with your hands to make sure it really gets mixed well. Stretch it and play with it yourself, just to make sure that it is the right consistency. Once you have mixed all of this in, then it is time to mix in your food coloring. Mix this in well, making sure it is evenly spread.

Once this is all mixed in, it is time to do the fun part! Throw in a ton of glitter and mix all of it in. Be careful not to get glitter everywhere, and do your best to really mix it in too. It is great to do a few different colors, in different bowls, so that your colors stay separated. It adds to the effect when the kids are playing with it, and I just find that it is beautiful.

If you are looking for an extra pop, then mix contrasting glitter into your slime, so mix silver glitter into the black slime and so on, to make sure that everything is fascinating, sparkly and fun to play with.

The kids had tons of fun playing with this. It is very fun to set up- just swirl around the different slimes together, making a big, colorful, sparkly slime tub. Once your kids start playing with it, the colors will start swirling and mixing together, creating a great visual experience.

Eventually, if you play with it for long enough, everything will mix together into one, big color. This is not necessarily a bad thing, as you will have lots of different colored glitter and a beautiful purple-blue colored slime that still shines like the night sky. Personally, I think that it is a win-win situation.

Your kids get plenty of sensory, fun play exploring a gorgeous galaxy of stars, and when they have finally mixed it all through, you are left with a stunning, reusable slime that you can keep playing with for days afterward.

This slime is another one which is pretty easy to store. Just pop it in an airtight container, and you are good to go. This slime should last for several weeks, so don't worry about it going bad.

As with most of these recipes, caution is advised, as it is not an edible slime, so little one should be very carefully supervised. Make sure that you watch your kids and don't let your younger ones play with the slime, unless you can be sure they won't ingest it.

Other than that, have fun and explore the galaxy with your kids in the comfort of your own home!

RECIPE 11- DOTTY SLIME

WE'VE shared a lot of slime recipes in this book, but this one might just be the most unusual slime. It follows the same, basic recipe as many other slimes, but it is a lot of fun since we've added another magic ingredient- dots!

Again, this is not a recipe that is safe for little children who still put everything in their mouths. This is a recipe for older children who understand instructions a little better, as the ingredients are not edible, and this means that this is not safe to eat.

That said, it is truly a fun recipe and a lot of fun to play with. The dots are a lot of fun to play with too, and they add a whole new level to the slime. This is especially true as they hold the slime together and help it stretch a lot better.

SUPPLIES:

- ½ cup liquid starch
- 5oz clear glue
- Lots of pom poms!

How to do it:

Put the glue into a bowl, and then slowly, slowly add the starch in, mixing all the while until you finally get to the consistency that you need. Make sure to keep mixing and make sure that you do so with your hands as well, in order to get it to a good consistency. Once you have done that, you need to add the pom poms and keep kneading them into the slime until it is workable consistency. Don't be scared to add plenty of pom poms as they really make this a fun slime to play with.

It is pretty easy to keep this slime, just put it in an air tight container, and you will be sure to keep the slime safe and good for plenty more uses. This slime keeps for several weeks, and it should not go bad, as there are no food products in it.

This is a great sensory activity and a good thing for kids to play and experiment with. It cleans off pretty easily, with soap and water. If you get it on carpets and fabric, you can wash it out using soap, water, and vinegar.

PLAY IDEAS

NOW that you have made your slime, there are so many things that you can use it for in order to enjoy it and make the most out of play time with your children. In the following part of the book, we will be discussing how you can use your slime for great playtime activities.

PLAY IDEA - 1

Giant slime bubbles! This is a fantastic way to really make the most of using your slime to have a lot of fun. It takes a few modifications to the traditional recipe to make this work, but it not too difficult to do. When you make your slime, you need to try and add a little more liquid starch to your mixture. This makes it a little bit more rubbery, which works perfectly for making giant bubbles.

Making slime bubbles is so much fun, and it is really easy to do.

Make sure that you add more liquid starch to your creation until it is more rubbery than it is slimy. If you pull it, it should stretch for a bit and then break off, unlike the usual slime consistency.

Once you have got the consistency right, it is only a simple matter to blow giant bubbles. Start off by getting a straw. The harder and wider your straw is the better this will work, but any straw will do in a pinch.

Roll your altered slime into a ball and stick your straw into it. Pinch the slime around the straw and then blow air into it. The air should expand the slime into a huge, solid bubble. These are so much fun to play with, and they hold their shape so well. Once they pop, you can just re-use the slime until you are finished with the activity.

This might be harder for the younger children to do, but most older kids will be able to get the hang of it pretty quickly. Don't worry if it takes you a few tries to get it right- it took me a while too! But once you have it figured out, you won't regret the time you took to figure this out.

Like most slimes, these giant bubbles are not really for little ones who still want to stick everything in their mouths. It is not edible or safe for them to have. But for older kids, this activity can keep them going all afternoon. It is so much fun to play outside, although the slime might not be as reusable after it falls in the dirt, you know?

So do whatever works for you and your family, but don't forget that giant slime bubbles can be a lot of fun if you are having a particularly boring day with the kids. It is also pretty helpful that the bubbles won't leave a slippery, dangerous residue on the floor, like most other bubble mixtures.

You can try and get the bubbles through hoops, or see who can keep the bubbles from popping the longest. The possibilities are pretty endless, and I am so happy to have found this idea!

PLAY IDEA - 2

Slime baskets are such an amazing way to use your slime. It is a pretty creative idea too because it involves more than just putting down a tub of slime. It allows for greater interaction of the slime, and a new sensory experience, which is so much fun to do.

Essentially, you need to make a good slime recipe that is not too runny, or too firm. Most of our slime recipes will work great for this method, but it's always a great idea to test and try different consistencies.

This activity is actually pretty self-explanatory. It is best done outside, but if you have a big indoor space, it would probably work too. Essentially, you need to grab a basket, such as a strawberry basket or a shopping basket. Hang it up over the kids' heads from a secure anchor point, and stick a tub underneath it.

What happens next is the really fun part. Just tip the slime into the basket and let gravity take its course. The slime should flow through the holes in the basket and fall into the tub in long, stretchy pieces that are so much fun for the kids to play with. It is also a good way to explain gravity.

Once all of the slimes has run through the holes, you can just grab the tub and tip the slime back into the basket. This activity can go on for ages, as the opportunities for play are almost endless. You can cut the slime, grab it, and have races with different bits of the slime and so much more. It is just a lot of fun to play with slime at such an unconventional angle, with most slime-based activities happening on the table or on the floor.

As you can tell, there is a good reason that we talk about the consistency so much. If it is too runny, it will slide through the holes far too quickly, and the kids won't get to actually experience it. However, if it is too tough and rubbery, then it won't flow properly, and you will have just as much of a problem.

Finding the right consistency is important, so experiment with the slime recipes above until one works for you. If you use the edible varieties, you might have to explore the possibilities of this a little longer to get it right.

We've had a lot of success with this one- my kids just love playing with it! So see if it works for you and your family, and I hope that you have as much fun with it as we did!

PLAY IDEA - 3

There are a few very cool things that you can do with slime that we haven't brought up yet. These are tips and tricks for those days where just playing with the slime isn't enough to entertain your kids. We definitely have those days, and sometimes they just need a little bit of extra-sensory assistance and activity to really stay entertained and engaged in the whole process.

Playing with cookie cutters. This is a really great way to play with slime. If you press them into the slime, you probably won't be left with neat little letters or shapes, but it is pretty great for the feel of it, and it looks really cool while you are doing it.

Add bits! Throw in toys and googly eyes and other little bits and pieces and have fun playing with them in the slime.

Make slime fart noises. Kids love fart noises, and they will find it hilarious if you teach them how to make an air pocket with the slime. This will definitely be a major hit.

Roll the slime into balls and see how long they can stay up. This is another really fun game to play with kids and helps them learn how to move quickly and improve motor skills. So it is a win-win all round.

Slime races! Push your slime up against a wall or another smooth surface such as tile, and see how long it takes for them to fall off. This can be quite a lot of fun, and it is a good way to experiment with the slime and what it can do. This is also another great way to really incorporate learning about gravity again.

Use tweezers to pick up slime. It is very slippery, and you probably won't have much success, but it is fantastic practice for fine motor skills, and it is a really good way to have a lot of fun and laughter too, while you are doing it.

If you can think of another use for slimy play time, then feel free to go for it. Just keep in mind that if you manage to get slime all over your clothing, it is best to soak it for at least 20 minutes in warm water to help dissolve the slime and make it easier to wash later. If it gets onto the carpets, vinegar, soap, and water work well at getting it off.

So have fun, experiment and get messy with your slimy creations!

PLAY IDEA - 4

We mentioned this in one of the earlier recipes, but slime is just such a great way to explore color theory and combining colors to make new ones. It is a splendid activity which combines both learning and fine motor skills. It is very fun to do, and I would highly recommend it to anyone who is looking to do a great activity with slime.

You can really spice this one up by adding scents to your slime or adding glitter and other pieces to the slime. This can help kids with creating meaningful combinations and learning about what works and what doesn't work in regards to combining colors and scents. For kids who are a little older, you can work on combining colors like blue and purple, or red and orange to create more subtle color variations.

This is a pretty great activity, and you can even use it in conjunction with other activities, such as the molten lava recipe, in order to make sure that you get the maximum playtime and learning time out of your slimy play.

Colors, scents, different shapes and sizes of glitter and so much more can be used to improve the whole experience, and it can be quite the learning experience for kids.

Also, it is fun for kids and parents alike, so why not jump right in?

TROUBLE SHOOTING YOUR SLIME

SO NOW we have covered a lot of different recipes that you can enjoy and experiment with. Most often, slime recipes will go well, and you will have a lot of fun playing with your slime (and so will your kids!). That said, slime recipes can go terribly wrong and, when they do, it can be hard to know what to do to fix the recipe.

In this section of the book, we have written a few good tips on how to really troubleshoot your slime if it goes wrong. We're talking about fixing lumpy slime, slime that is too rubbery, slime that is too watery and more. So if you have any issues with your slime, you have come to the right spot!

We have decided to focus on the most common recipe in this section, the liquid starch/ glue combination that we have used in many of our recipes. Some of our tips might seem a little bit obvious, and some won't, so hopefully, you will find the answer you are looking for in between. I have had to go through so much trial and error to make sure that we have a few great recipes, and I think I must have gone through at least 100 bottles of glue!

To start with it is important always to check that your glue is up to date and that you have shaken your liquid starch really well to ensure that nothing has sunk to the bottom of the container or bottle.

Stringy, Watery, Sticky Slime

If your starch is stringy, watery and not really working at all, then you have probably not added enough liquid starch. This is quite a common problem, and it can lead to slime that doesn't stick together properly, doesn't have that lovely, rubbery texture that slime seems to get. Of course, you don't want it too rubbery either; you want it just right!

If this is your problem, then don't worry- it is a pretty easy fix! Just add more liquid starch to your mix. This needs to be done slowly, adding a little bit at a time and making sure that you mix it in really well. Sometimes, it can help to mix it in with your hands as well, to make sure that you get the consistency that you are looking for. If you are stirring and you can lift a good portion of your slime (instead of stringy little bits), then you can be sure that you have done a pretty good job in fixing your slime and making the most of your mixture.

Stringy Slime That Does Not Stick

If you have slime that is stringy and lumpy, but just does not stick to anything, then you have probably added too much liquid starch and not enough glue. This can look terrible, and it feels even worse.

The first thing to do is to drain the mixture of any standing liquid starch that you see. Then you need to add glue slowly and gradually, stirring the whole time. Once you have made sure that it is as mixed as it is going to get with a spoon, then it is time to mix it by hand. If you still have trouble after that, then you might benefit from letting it rest in an airtight container overnight.

Your slime is ready to go when it sticks together and isn't stringy or watery. It should be pretty smooth and even, and it should stretch well. Once you have gotten your slime to this consistency, then you know that you have achieved what you have set out to do.

This slime will keep for many weeks, as long as you seal it in an airtight container, so that it does not dry out and get gross. This slime is amazing to play with, as are all the recipes that we have covered above and can provide hours and hours of entertainment.

If You Get It On Yourself

A good wash with soap and water will get this off your skin without any issues. It is pretty easy to clean off, although a bath is sometimes needed after playing!

If You Get It On Plastic/ Glass/ Wood

If you get it on the above surfaces, it should clean off pretty easily with soap and water, just like if you get it onto your skin. The key to getting it off easily is to make sure that you don't let it dry. Just clean it off straight away, and it will be okay.

If You Get It On Fabric

If you get it on your clothing, then it is pretty easy to clean it by soaking it in warm water for at least 20 minutes, then putting it through the washing machine. If you get it on the carpet, spray it with vinegar, before cleaning it off with soap and water. Thankfully, it is a pretty easy slime to clean out of your fabrics!

I hope this helped you with troubleshooting your slime and making the perfect batch every time!

Part 2

How to Make Putty

HOW TO MAKE PUTTY

MAking slime is a lot of fun, but making putty can be equally or sometimes more rewarding and will ensure that your kids have plenty to play with, especially when the holidays strike. Upon looking for how to make slime, I stumbled upon quite a few putty recipes instead. I am so glad that I filed them away instead of ignoring them, because they have come in handy for those days when the kids needed a little extra entertainment, and we'd exhausted our list of slime activities.

This is also great for kids who struggle with the sensory difficulties posed by slime. Slime can be very, very messy and, well, slimy! Some kids find that hard to manage, and putty is a more workable alternative for them. If you don't want the same mega-clean up as slime brings, then this is another really great way to get them playing and squishing, without the same, huge mess. All up, this is a pretty good way to bust boredom and get your kids engaged in the activities again.

RECIPE 1- BASIC PUTTY RECIPE

THE MOST basic recipe that I found is one that works in a similar way to the original slime recipes. You need liquid starch, just like before, and you also need to get some standard school glue. However, instead of grabbing the clear glue, which is stickier and stretchier, you need to find the regular white glue, which will work so much better for this particular recipe.

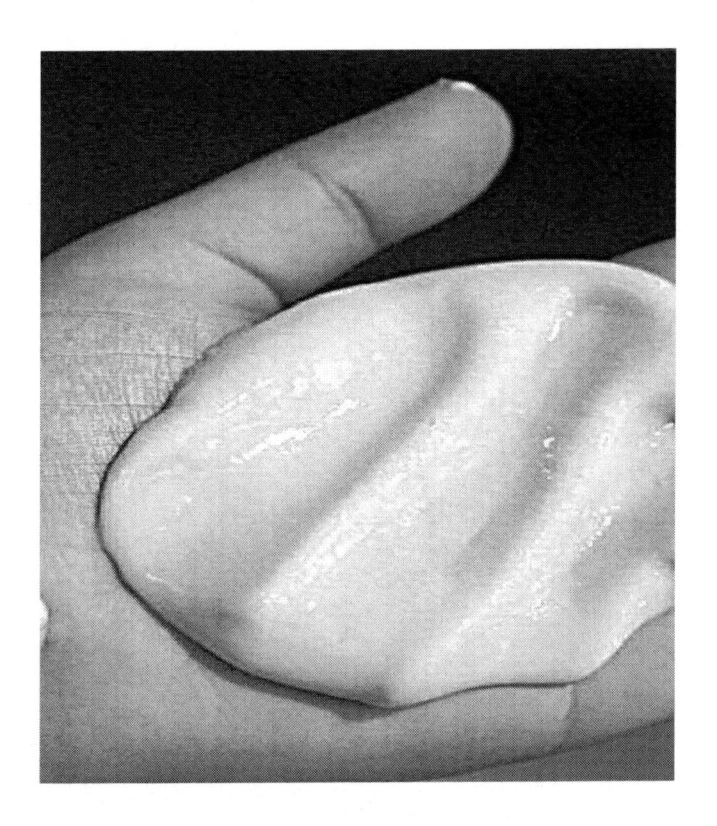

Supplies:

- 5 oz. White glue
- ½ cup liquid starch.
- Food coloring

How to do it:

Once you have gathered all of your supplies, the rest of this procedure is really similar to all of our slime recipes. First, add the food coloring to your liquid starch and really mix it up so that it is even in coloring. Once you have done this, you need to put your glue in a bowl. Slowly add your liquid starch to the glue and mix it in, continuing to add the liquid starch slowly in order to make sure that it mixes to an even consistency. This is vital to make sure that it mixes properly.

Remember that this time, you are trying to achieve the consistency of silly putty, instead of slime. This is a far more stable consistency- it is not as sticky or as runny as slime. It needs to be stretchy, but more likely to break off in your hands if you stretch it for too far.

Once you have mixed it with a spoon, you can mix it with your hands until you get the right consistency. This is a really great way to make sure that you get the mix right, as the consistency you feel once it had been stretched by hand, will help you judge if you have the right consistency.

Keep rolling it around and stretching it until all of the colors has dispersed evenly and you find that it is the consistency you need and want.

My kids were thrilled when I gave them the putty. It really is a lot easier to clean up, so they were allowed to play with it in the lounge room, over a big tub. This is unusual, as our lounge is carpeted, but it was so much fun to break the usual routine and do something a little more novel.

They had a lot of fun actually getting into it, stretching it and pulling it and molding it into different shapes. Because it is silly putty, you can't expect it to hold its shape, as well as play dough, does, but it does hold its shape a lot better than slime. This in-between experience was new for them, and they had great fun exploring with it.

Once you have finished playing, all you need to do is store it in a container that is air tight. It should keep for many weeks, much like the slimes. It is a good one to have on hand for those rainy days, where you would prefer to stay inside, but still, want to have the sensory goodness of this type of play.

Clean up is really easy. If any putty has escaped, just clean it up and put it back in its container. Get your children to wash their hands with soap and water, and clean up any extra mess with either soap and water or a little bit of vinegar.

Please keep in mind that the ingredients in this particular recipe are definitely not edible, so you should keep your younger children well away from this particular activity. Even older children should be supervised to make sure they no putty gets put into their mouths.

Other than that, it is fun, simple and not quite as messy as slime, which is a bit of a win all-around!

RECIPE 2- LAUNDRY DETERGENT PUTTY

MOST of us tend to have some sort of glue on hand at all times in our homes. That said, not everyone has liquid starch running around their house. If you are looking for a rainy day activity that you need to whip up quick, then a trip to the store might just seem a little bit out of your reach, especially if you have two tired or fed-up children who are not in the best space to leave the house.

If you have ever found yourself in this situation (I know that I have!), then you are going to love this recipe. It focuses on using things that most of us have in our homes at any given moment, so you should be able to whip on up even if you have restless kids under foot.

SUPPLIES:

¼ cup white glue

2 Tablespoons of laundry detergent

HOW TO DO IT:

For this recipe, you can use as much or as little of the glue and detergent as you like, just make sure that you adjust the amounts accordingly. You can do this recipe with either liquid laundry detergent or with powder. Both of them will work okay, although you might have to stir the powdered detergent a little more and a little longer.

Add the glue first, putting it into a bowl. Then stir in the food coloring, making sure that it is mixed in very evenly into the mixture. Then slowly begin adding the detergent. You will need to mix this very well. Keep adding detergent until you are happy with the consistency, and you can see it beginning to bond together like silly putty should.

Once you have mixed it all in well with a spoon, then it is time to start mixing it in by hand. Make sure that you really knead the mixture until it forms a smooth and even consistency. This might take some time, and you really need to stretch and roll this one around for a while to let it reach the right consistency.

When you are finished, just pop it into an airtight container and let it sit in the fridge for ten minutes to an hour. This will help it set so that it is ready to play with. When you take it out of the fridge, make sure you warm it up by kneading it for a minute or too, before giving it to your kids.

This was such a huge hit in our home! The kids could not tell the difference between this recipe and the one that used liquid starch, and they loved them both equally. I dare say that this one smelt better, though! Liquid starch has a pretty strong scent, while this recipe just smelt like soap and detergent, which is a smell that I personally like quite a lot.

It has a good consistency, quite stretchy and fun to play with! My kids enjoyed it too, so this is definitely a recipe I will be keeping on hand.

When it comes to playing, this one is not too messy, but still, try and keep it in a tub, so that play doesn't end up messing the carpets too badly. As with most recipes that contain soaps, this is obviously not edible, so you need to make sure you keep an eye on younger children who might be tempted to put this in their mouths. It is good to pay attention to even older kids, and just watch out that none of the putties is eaten or tasted. Detergent is definitely not a good thing to be chewing on!

Clean up is pretty simple, just soap, water, and vinegar on fabrics. Your kids probably won't need a bath after this activity, which is a pretty big plus in my personal opinion!

RECIPE 3- BORAX PUTTY

MOST of the recipes that we have covered this far have not contained Borax. That is because even though Borax is pretty great when it comes to making an amazing putty or slime, it is also dangerous when it comes to ingesting it. I mean, sure, it is not good to eat glue or starch, but it's a little bit more forgiving than Borax.

All of that said, it is still a really good ingredient when it comes to making good silly putty. It's a little more complex than most of these recipes, but I hope you will stay with me while I go over it- it is worth it! So in this particular recipe, we will be covering how to make a great borax putty.

SUPPLIES:

2 oz. white glue

¼ cup water

1 tablespoon Borax

1/8 cup water

Food coloring

How to do it:

The first step to this recipe is taking your glue and mixing it with ¼ cup of water. You need to mix it really well and make sure it is an even consistency before you even consider going onto the next step. If you want food coloring, then now is a good time to add it to your recipe. Again, mix it until the mixture has an even color that you like.

Now comes the trickier bit! You need to dissolve your borax in 1/8 cup of water, making sure that it is completely dissolved in order to make sure that the putty does not have yucky flecks or grainy bits in it.

Slowly pour your borax mixture into your glue, slowly stirring until it begins to bond together. Continue to stir and add until your mixture starts to look right, and at the consistency of silly putty. When you see this, then it is time to start mixing with your hands. You need to mix it well at this stage, pulling and stretching it until it is the consistency that you want.

Mixing is the key to many of these recipes, as it is a very important part of making sure that your putty is pliable and a good consistency.

My kids are old enough to be trusted not to put things into their mouths if I ask them not to, so I was happy to let them play with this recipe. They really liked it, as it had a pretty fun stretch to it. They didn't complain about it being grainy, so I must have mixed it up well enough for their liking.

It is a pretty good putty, as it holds its shape quite nicely, has enough stretch to be fun, but is not too sticky. When we were finished playing, we just put it back into an airtight container.

I decided to store it in the fridge until we needed it next time, and it stored really well. When I took it out the next time, it wasn't really pliable, but after I played with it and kneaded it for about ten minutes, it was right as rain and ready to be played with again.

This goes without saying, but when you are finished playing with this putty, it is super important to wash your hands and make sure that your kids do the same. It is not safe to ingest Borax, and you don't really want it rubbed into eyes either. For this reason, make sure you wash your hands well, with soap and water, and clean up the area that you used for play.

Aside from that, as long as you keep it in an airtight container, and well away from kids who might be inclined to put toys and fingers in their mouths, then this recipe doesn't pose any threat. You know your kids and what they are and are not ready for, so I am sure I don't need to tell you this.

On a plus note- this putty holds its color really nicely, and you get a really bright putty to play with!

RECIPE 4- BABY POWDER PUTTY

IF YOU are looking for a putty with a slightly different consistency, then this one might be a good option. It has a gentle stretch, and it doesn't bounce. It feels a little bit more like clay, but my kids still really enjoyed this putty, and it was a nice break from the type of sensory play we have been engaging in lately.

The recipe is also pretty simple, and it smells great!

Supplies:

- 5 Tablespoons baby powder
- 1 Teaspoon of white glue

How to do it:

First, you need to scoop out five tablespoons of baby powder into a bowl. Add one teaspoon of white glue to the mixture, and then begin to mix it in well. It should mix quite nicely and without too much trouble, but you might find yourself needing to knead it by hand. If it is too powdery and dry, add a little bit more glue until it is at the consistency that you desire.

It is a little messy to start mixing it, as the baby powder tends to go everywhere. But once you have gotten the consistency you want, and have mixed all the powder through, then it really turns into a great slime for play time.

The one great bonus about this slime is the fact that it smells just like baby powder, which is amazing. It is not really advised to add a lot of food coloring and other additives to this particular putty, because of the use of baby powder. Food coloring can make it patchy and alter the consistency, so it is better just to stick to the very basics with this one.

Even though baby powder and glue are not as dangerous as the more chemical-orientates putties, it is still not very wise to ingest this, or even taste it. It is not edible, so keep it away from little ones who want to eat everything.

This putty is a lot of fun to play with. It does not have much of a stretchy texture, and it is not sticky, which makes it great when you want to minimize mess during play and ensure that your kids are getting exposed to a lot of different textures, rather than just one type of putty.

We found this was great fun, and it is easy to clean with just soap and water. It is actually easier to clean than most other putties that we have tried so far because it is not so sticky. You can vacuum it out of the carpet, and soak clothes in some hot water to get rid of any residue.

RECIPE 5- SOAP PUTTY

THIS was a really interesting recipe to try. I found that the consistency was slightly more like a slime consistency, but that it was still great to use as silly putty. I had not used or even heard of this recipe until recently, but I could not resist trying it. It is pretty simple in reality, and you likely have these ingredients in your home already.

SUPPLIES:

- Soap (body wash or liquid soap)
- Shampoo

HOW TO DO IT:

Combine equal parts of your liquid soap with your shampoo. Make sure that you mix this up well before you put in a resealable bag. Put this bag in the fridge overnight, or, if you are in a hurry, put it in the freezer for a couple of hours.

This will allow for the soap and shampoo to congeal nicely and form into a great silly putty that is so much fun to play with.

This one is really messy, just a word of warning! It is a lot of fun to play with though, so just make sure you do it in a tub or outside. One of the great plusses to this one is that it is perfectly safe to play with in the bath!

If your kids get this all over themselves and in the water, you can just consider it to be an extra bath for them!

We actually found this was an amazing bath time activity, as we could play with it in a tub, then get into the bath and play with it some more, watching it dissolve and form bubbles depending on how it was played with. This is not something that we ever thought we would be able to do with a slime, so to find this one was so great!

It is not quite as firm as most putties, but it smells utterly amazing, and it has so many uses that it is hard not to love it. If you do decide that you want to keep it and not play with it in the bath, then it will store well in an airtight container, in the fridge.

As we mentioned before, clean-up is really easy, just use water, and it will wash right off without any problem. It will even wash out of fabrics and carpets with a limited amount of fuss. Since these are soap products, try and avoid letting your kids eat them, or get them in their eyes. Other than that, play is pretty easy and simple and a heck of a lot of fun! This recipe was definitely a hit with our family.

RECIPE 6- SOAP AND FLOUR

THIS recipe was similar to the one we did before with baby powder. It is a really cool recipe if you are looking for something a little bit different, which uses ingredients that you already have around the house.

The texture is a little more stretchy and pliable than the recipe we did with the baby powder, and it is a lot of fun to work with. Then again, we try and make sure that all of our recipes are fun since that is the point of play time!

SUPPLIES:

- Flour
- Liquid soap/ shower gel

HOW TO DO IT:

This is another super easy recipe. All you need to do is add one part flour to the bowl and slowly add one part liquid soap to the mix. Slowly stir it in until it is the consistency that you want. Then it is time to get messy! Mix it in with your hands, taking your time to make sure all of the flour is mixed in well, and that it is an even consistency. Unlike the baby powder recipe, you can add food coloring to this one to add a little bit of fun to your activity.

This is a pretty great recipe. My kids were not quite as interested in it, but we recently did the baby powder recipe, so that is probably why. I found it to have a really great consistency, and it is another putty that smells amazing, just like my favorite body wash (since that is what I used).

Even though there is flour in this one, it is still not an edible putty, and you need to keep it away from younger kids. That said, it is pretty easy to clean up since it is just flour and soap. A good scrub with warm water will get it off almost anything, so try and not limit the play too much.

It is a lot of fun to play with, and once I played with it for a while, the kids warmed up to the idea and started playing with me.

So if you are looking for a quick slime that is not too sticky, then this can be an excellent alternative.

RECIPE 7- GLITTER PUTTY

GLITTER Putty sounded like such a fun idea that I just had to try it! The putty that we made is gold in color, which we achieved by using a ton of gold glitter and some yellow food coloring, with just a tiny touch of orange food coloring. It worked out so well that I am really excited to see what else we can do with the putty! At first, I was a little bit skeptical, but it turns out that it works just as well as it does in slime, if not better!

The supplies are the same as our basic putty recipe, with the addition of glitter.

Supplies:

- 5 oz. White glue
- ½ cup liquid starch.
- Food coloring
- Glitter!

How to do it:

First, add the food coloring to your liquid starch and really mix it up so that it is even in coloring. Make sure to add more yellow than orange, as you are looking for a gold color, rather than a dark yellow or light orange. Once you have done this, you need to put your glue in a bowl. Slowly add your liquid starch to the glue and mix it in, continuing to add the liquid starch slowly in order to make sure that it mixes to an even consistency. This is crucial to make sure that it mixes properly.

After this, just add a lot of glitters! Be warned; this is where it really gets messy if you are not careful. You need to use fine glitter, so be careful not to let it get everywhere. Glitter is so hard to clean, after all!

Once you have mixed it with a spoon, you can mix it with your hands until you get the right consistency. When you are done, you should be left with golden, glittery slime that just looks so amazing!

My kids really, really loved this one, and I don't blame them. It has the consistency of your usual putty, but it really does sparkle and shine, which is something we really like in this family. Wash up is easy as long as you are careful when you are mixing in the glitter since that is where things are most likely to get messy.

As with most of these, it is not safe to eat, so watch your younger kids. The fact that it is so shiny can be pretty tempting so that I would watch like a hawk around play time. Other than that, this experiment was so much fun, and I think it worked out well!

RECIPE 8- RAINBOW PUTTY

AFTER the success of our rainbow slime, I just had to try Rainbow Putty, and I was not disappointed.

I think it works even better than rainbow slime for mixing colors, as you can be a lot more precise. This is especially great for older kids who understand color theory a little bit already.

Making this putty was pretty easy and didn't take too much effort or time. Start with a basic putty recipe.

SUPPLIES:

- 5 oz. White glue
- ½ cup liquid starch.
- Food coloring (lots of colors!)

HOW TO DO IT:

First, add the food coloring to your liquid starch and mix it up so that it is even in coloring. Once you have done this, you need to put your glue in a bowl. Slowly add your liquid starch to the glue and mix it in, continuing to add the liquid starch slowly in order to make sure that it mixes to an even consistency. It is important to note that you will probably need quite a few bowls, to make lots of different batches of your putty. Only put one color in each bowl, to keep the colors clear and bright.

Colors will not be as vivid as they were with the slime since you are using white glue. That said, they should still pop enough to entice your kids to play with them.

Once you have mixed it with a spoon, you can mix it with your hands until you get the right consistency. Then just keep mixing and having fun! My kids spent ages with these putties, mixing, creating and experimenting.

If they all get mixed together, then you still have a pretty decent putty to play with. Maybe add some glitter to make it more appealing, and then pop it into a container which is airtight, in order to play with it later on.

This was definitely a great experiment, and I would play with rainbow slime any day!

PLAY IDEAS

SILLY putty is just so much fun to play with on its own that you might not need any extra ideas. That said, if you find yourself needing to do more to occupy your children's time, then here are the best ideas that I have found, to help you bust the boredom and get the most out of your putty.

SILLY PUTTY PLAY IDEAS 1- SILLY PUTTY IN A BAG

Playing with putty in a bag is an amazing way to really get the most of your play time. This is an especially helpful way to play with silly putty if you are looking to improve motor skills and sensory tolerance.

Fill the bag with lots of little objects, like sequins, and then add your putty, before you seal the bag off. Playing with the sparkly sequins and working through the putty is a lot of fun and is a different and unusual way to play with putty that your kids will probably love!

Try and use fingers to write or draw on the putty through your sealed bag. This is interesting as it gives kids an idea of pressure and how to make their shapes last. Also, it is a heck of a lot of fun to try and do it quickly.

Draw mazes on the bag, and put a bead inside the bag, with the putty. Your child can try and push the bead through the maze. If that sounds too complicated, just draw a shape and have them push the bead in and out of shape.

Using a marker to draw a shape on the side of your bag is a lovely way to start the play. Make sure you use a good quality zip lock bag so that your child does not run the risk of making a mess (through no fault of their own). It can be a lot of fun to try and get all of the putties to fit inside the shape that you have drawn, and it is a really good way to engage the fine motor skills.

Put bits of foam inside your putty to try and create shapes or faces. You can also hide pictures and words, even little foam letters to push around the bag and try and make sense of what is inside.

SILLY PUTTY PLAY IDEAS 1- SILLY PUTTY OUT OF A BAG

YOU can use silly putty in a similar way to slime when it comes to color theory. Using putty instead of slime lets you child have more control over mixing the colors. If you like, you can even mix the colors in a more subtle way, to show your child more of the color spectrum.

This is a great way to teach them about the more subtle increments in color and is great for older kids who already know their basic color wheel.

Another really fun way to play with putty is to put a big amount in a bowl or tub and hide things within it for your children to find. This can be a lot of fun, and you can have races to see who can find the most "bits" inside the putty.

If that does not appeal to you, putty is great for imaginative play- just add a few plastic toys, and you have a whole new adventure for your children's favorite characters.

In conclusion- putty is a great way to play. It is less messy than slime but has an amazing teachable range and so many great recipes to use.

If you are stuck on what to do with your kids, try a putty recipe. It is good for indoor play, easy to wash out and provides lots of fun and sensory development.

I hope you and your family get just as much enjoyment out of putty as me and my kids have!

Part 3

How to Make a Liquid Rainbow

HOW TO MAKE LIQUID RAINBOWS

I JUST want to take the opportunity to say that Liquid Rainbows are the coolest! They look amazing, and they are such a great way to get kids excited about science. It is a really good learning opportunity as it teaches so many cool things.

It teaches kids about viscosity, as well as density. It also teaches kids about different liquids, different colors and it encourages a steady hand for pouring.

So if you are looking for a break from the messy play that arises from slime and putty, this might be a good alternative.

It is a lot of fun and pretty easy to do. Added to that, it is also pretty quick to do, so you should be able to hold your kids' attention. So without further ado, let us move onto the recipe!

RECIPE

Supplies:

- Food coloring
- Oil (olive oil works well, but most other oils will work just fine as well)
- Rubbing alcohol
- Corn syrup
- Blue dish soap

How to do it:

The actual process isn't hard, per say, it just takes precision and a fairly slow and steady hand. You might have to help your kids with the steps, but talking through the process is part of the learning experience.

Purple

Start with your corn syrup. This is the liquid which is the densest of the lot. This means that it will stay at the bottom and hold its position really well. Color it purple, mixing it all up in a container. Then pour it very slowly into a long, thin container.

Blue

This is where the blue dish soap comes in handy! Mix some into a cup (we recommend about ½ a cup per color), and then pour it very slowly down the side of the glass container that holds the purple layer. This is where it is super important to go slowly. If you take it really slowly, you won't get a mixing of the layers. If you go too quickly, the layers will mix, and you won't get the desired effect. Doing it slowly is the key to success for this one.

Green

Green is the next step in the process. This is where you use water and food coloring. Use green food coloring to color the liquid, before slowly, slowly pouring the water down, along the side of the glass. Like always, you need to go really slowly to make sure that there is no mixing. You should have three layers now, and you can start to see the rainbow effect forming!

Yellow

This layer uses oil. If the oil is already yellow in color, then there is no need to color it. Simply pour it very slowly down the side of the glass to make your next layer. Of course, you know this already, but going slowly is really helpful at this part. Make sure that none of the layers mix together, and you will be alright. This is really one of my favorite bits- it looks so lovely!

Red

This is the last layer, and it is one of the trickiest one to do. Color the alcohol, and the slowly, slowly pour it down the sides of the glass. This layer can be tricky as the layer before it is susceptible to being broken. Once you are finished, you should have a completed rainbow in a glass!

Liquid Rainbows are so beautiful, and they provide a great way to talk about science with your kids. Keep in mind that the lighter the color is, the better it will look. When you put all of the colors together, they tend to darken, and they do not look as good. Make sure you spend time getting the right tone, color, and consistency so that this does not happen.

Other than that, I find that this is a pretty straightforward and easy activity to do with your children, and is quite a lot of fun to do. I hope you have the same success that we have been lucky enough to have with this one!

PLAY IDEAS (AND WHAT TO TALK ABOUT!)

THERE are many ways that you can incorporate science into this activity, so I thought I would compile a few of the options in this part of the book. It is very important to consider talking about science and learning while doing this, as it is so easy to sneak it in!

To start with, you can talk about measurement. Your child can help you measure out the right amount (1/2 a cup) per color. This is a fairly simple activity for older kids, but take it slow for the younger ones. You can also teach older children about halves and counting, by adding one-half and one-half, to make a whole. This is a good way to bring maths into your day and easily work it into the activity.

That said, that is not the only thing that can be discussed while you are making amazing rainbows. You can also talk about density. Talk about which liquid feels thicker, and what density means. You can talk about how we know a liquid is dense and what that means. Focus on why the other liquids do not sink through or mix with the first liquids that you put into the container.

On that note, you can talk about viscosity and the differences between the liquids. These are amazing things to talk about. Talk about it even if your children are young because it is good to expose them to the information, even if they do not fully understand it yet.

For younger children, you can start talking about color theory, how the different colors mix to create a new color. Start with red and blue, mixing them together to create purple, and so forth.

If you are looking for a little something extra, then grab a few little items from around your home and see which ones sink, which ones float and which ones get stuck in the middle. Drop a few different weights and see where they land. Then you can talk about the density with your children again, mentioning that if the liquid is denser than the object, the object will get 'stuck.'

I had a lot of fun playing with the rainbow with my kids, and they loved dropping things through the colors and seeing where they would land!

Now, while this is a gorgeous rainbow, and is really great to play with, keep in mind that this is definitely not drinkable! It can be tempting for kids, especially since it is in a glass, so make sure you let them know that they cannot drink this. The alcohol on the top will pose a serious risk to children (being rubbing alcohol), so make sure you have a big talk with your children before you play, and ensure that little children are kept well away from the mixture.

If you want to add some extra interest once the activity is finished, have your kids decorate the jar, adding stickers and other objects to the glass to increase craft time and make it all the more beautiful.

If you have any twinkle lights or small lights, drape them over the glass container, or tuck them behind to create a gorgeous light show. This is a lot of fun, and my kids wanted me to leave it in the room while they slept, they liked it so much!

Unfortunately for them (and for me), this is a perishable substance, so it is not safe to leave it lying around. Your rainbow probably won't last very long, because of the oil and corn syrup. You might be able to keep it for a day or so, but then you need to throw it away, which is unfortunate.

As a last experiment, I put it into a sealable bottle and shook it around, mixing it all up. I will say that it looked absolutely amazing, as most of the colors stay separate as little bubbles, although some of them do mix with interesting color results!

The colors didn't separate back to their layers, though, and once we had finished the experiment, we tipped it down the drain and cleaned out all the containers.

That said, we had so much fun playing with it, and it really looked lovely for the day or so that we kept it, even with the ping pong ball floating at the top!

So if you are looking for a little science experiment that is both fun and seriously educational, then this might be a good option for you and your family. Don't worry about getting it perfect- you can always try again.

And if you are bored with the rainbow, how about layering it with stripes, or seeing what other color combinations you can come up with? Are there any other liquids that work well? Experiment, have fun and let your kids explore the different viscosities.

Just try not to taste the rainbow!

CONCLUSION

THANK you for coming along with my kids for this wild ride and me! Crafting and creating is just so, so important to do, especially for those families who have young kids! This is a lovely way to embrace children's natural creativity and curiosity and make the most of it.

In this book, we have covered so many different types of sensory play, which can be found in slimes and putties. We have also explored the use of find motor skills and how playing with slime and putty can actually be really helpful for children learning to grip things properly. Not only that but combining colors and engaging in pretend/ imaginative play is just so important for kids, no matter what their ages are.

I know that some of the recipes in this book are messy, and I hope that clean-up is just as fun as playing. Be it an extra-long bath, or clean-up time for the whole family, I hope that you enjoy it. Soap and water will work for most of the recipes, and if they don't, then some good old vinegar and a long soak will deal with the rest.

Hopefully, in between all of the madness, you have found some ideas and inspiration for your own crazy concoctions and adventures. I am really honored that you took the time to read through all of my anecdotes, my recipes, my ramblings and my musings.

My kids and I have had so much fun testing all of these recipes and working through play. I hope that, if nothing else, it was an entertaining read. But, at best, I hope that this was informative and that it will help you and your kids have fun.

Never underestimate how important it is for children to have fun, to engage with their world, and to really explore everything that the world has to offer in regards to textures, smells, colors and experiences.

So thank you for taking time out of your busy, busy schedule as a parent, to read and learn about these things! I am by no means an expert, but I hope that by sharing my experiences, I can reach out and help your family in some small way.

Remember that you are doing an incredible job and that no one is perfect- no one needs to be. Your kids appreciate you for who you are, and you are doing a fantastic job. Remember that no matter what challenges you face as a family, you can get through them all with patience and love. And, when life allows for it- a heck of a lot of laughter!

I wish you all the best, and I hope your children enjoy the recipes.

Stay Messy! Have Fun!

Made in the USA
San Bernardino, CA
15 May 2017